Miffy Goes Ice-Skating!

Based on the work of **Dick Bruna**
Story written by **Maggie Testa**

SIMON SPOTLIGHT

New York London Toronto Sydney New Delhi

SIMON SPOTLIGHT
An imprint of Simon & Schuster Children's Publishing Division
1230 Avenue of the Americas, New York, New York 10020
This Simon Spotlight paperback edition August 2017
Published in 2017 by Simon & Schuster, Inc.
Publication licensed by Mercis Publishing bv, Amsterdam.
Stories and images are based on the work of Dick Bruna.
'Miffy and Friends' © copyright Mercis Media bv, all rights reserved.
All rights reserved, including the right of reproduction in whole or in part in any form.
SIMON SPOTLIGHT and colophon are registered trademarks of Simon & Schuster, Inc.
For information about special discounts for bulk purchases, please contact Simon & Schuster Special Sales
at 1-866-506-1949 or business@simonandschuster.com.
Manufactured in the United States of America 0717 LAK
10 9 8 7 6 5 4 3 2 1
ISBN 978-1-5344-0419-9 (pbk)
ISBN 978-1-5344-0420-5 (eBook)

Miffy is going ice-skating today! Barbara promised she would take her skating when Miffy got her new ice skates.

But when Miffy knocks on Barbara's door, no one answers. Instead, she hears a tapping sound. Where could it be coming from?

The tapping is coming from Boris's workshop!

"Hi, Boris," Miffy greets him. "What are you making today?"

"I'm just mending this chair," Boris tells her.

"Is Barbara here?" Miffy asks. "She said when I got my new ice skates she'd teach me how to spin."

"Sorry, Miffy," Boris answers. "Barbara's gone shopping. I'm sure she'd love to take you another day." Miffy sighs. "Okay. Bye then, Boris."

Boris has an idea. "You could stay and help me fix the chair if you like."

Miffy likes the sound of that! "And then maybe you could take me ice-skating?" she suggests. Boris agrees.

Boris has a special song to help him finish the chair.
He teaches it to Miffy:

*"You have to
Get yourself ready.
Keep everything steady.
It takes time to get it right!"*

Boris and Miffy finish fixing the chair in no time!
"Now we can go ice-skating!" says Miffy happily,
and they head outside.

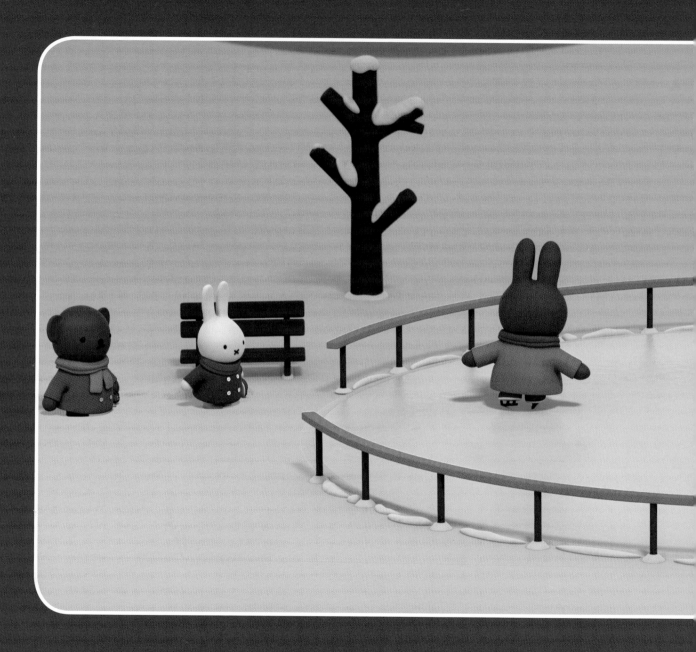

It isn't long before Miffy and Boris arrive at the rink.
Miffy can't wait to join the other skaters on the ice.

But first she must put on her new ice skates.

She laces them up really tightly before she steps onto the ice.

"Come on," she calls to Boris.

Miffy is a good skater. "Skating is such fun!" she says to Boris from the ice.

"I'm coming," Boris assures her. "Give me a moment. I'm just checking to see if my skates are on properly."

Miffy skates over to Boris. "They look fine to me," Miffy says. "Come on, Boris! This way!"

"Whee!" Miffy calls as she skates away.

"Okay, here goes," says Boris.

But Boris is unsteady on his feet. He starts to wobble . . . and then wobble some more. . . .

And then he falls down!

"Boris, what happened?" Miffy asks.
"I'm sorry, Miffy," says Boris. "I don't know how to ice-skate."
"Here, let me help you up," says Miffy.

Miffy has an idea! "I know how you can learn to skate!"

Miffy leaves the ice for a moment. When she returns, she has the chair she and Boris worked on. Boris holds on to the chair and pushes off.

Miffy sings Boris's song back to him.

"You have to
Get yourself ready.
Keep everything steady.
It takes time to get it right!"

Boris is skating in no time!
"I really enjoy skating now, all thanks to you!" Boris
tells Miffy.

"You're welcome, Boris," says Miffy. "And now you can watch my skating show!"

Miffy glides across the ice, skates backward, and even does a spin!

Well done, Miffy!